THE DOVE
AND THE
MESSIAH

THE DOVE AND THE MESSIAH

based on a legend often told at Christmastime among the people of Mexico

adapted and retold by
Dorothy Van Woerkom

illustrated by
Art Kirchhoff

Concordia
Publishing House
St. Louis   London

To my parents
Helen and Peter O'Brien

Concordia Publishing House, St. Louis, Missouri
Concordia Publishing House Ltd., London, E. C. 1
Copyright © 1975 Concordia Publishing House

Manufactured in the United States of America

Library of Congress Cataloging in Publication Data

Van Woerkom, Dorothy.
    The dove and the Messiah.

    SUMMARY: A Mexican legend explaining how the dove
became the symbol for the Holy Spirit.
    (1. Folklore—Mexico. 2. Christmas stories)
I. Kirchhoff, Art. II. Title.
PZ8.1.V457Do   232.9'21 (E)   75-9607
ISBN 0-570-03450-7

PREFACE

Long, long ago, simple-hearted people who felt close to God tried to explain the world around them through religious stories, or legends.

When the early Christian Mexicans heard the sad cry of the mourning dove from its roost in the *cañada*, they wondered why it mourned so. One day someone made up a legend, telling of a dove who mourned because she never saw the Christ Child—and of how it was that the dove became our symbol for the Holy Spirit.

The wind heard it first. "The Messiah is coming!" an angel had said. "Blow the glad tidings all around the universe."

"The Messiah is coming!" the wind told the stars as it swept in and out among them. "Give the message to the planets as they pass."

And then, with a rush and a rustle the wind told the beasts of the forests and the creeping things along the riverbanks. At the ocean's edge it told the seagulls.

"The Messiah is coming!" roared the wind. "Tell the birds of the land and the creatures beneath the sea."

Up the mountain sped a gull to tell the eagle. The eagle swooped low along the lake and told the swan. The swan called to a swallow flying overhead, and the swallow hurried off to tell the nighthawk. In the darkest hour of night, the nighthawk told the owl.

Soon all the creatures on the earth and in the air and in the sea had heard the tidings.

All, that is, except the dove. She was quiet and shy. She lived alone in her home in the cliff, and the other birds forgot about her.

At last, on a winter's midnight, the owl saw the Star. He heard the angels' voices fill the sky. He saw the shepherds leave their flocks and hurry down the hillside.

The owl followed after them. He followed them through the sleeping town, into the quiet yard behind an inn. There, from a cave where animals sheltered, came a great and blinding light. The owl blinked against the brightness. He made his way to a niche in the wall near the roof of the cave.

Below, in a straw-filled manger lay a child. The shepherds knelt before Him in awe and adoration. Above them, unseen and silent, the owl worshiped also.

And in a little while the shepherds hurried away to spread the wondrous news among their friends.

On swift, strong wings the owl returned to the leafy darkness of his tree to await the dawn.

"The Messiah has come!" the owl told the lark at daybreak. "I have seen Him. He lies at Bethlehem beneath that great, bright Star!"

The lark spread the news, and soon all the birds were winging their way to the holy town. Below them came the beasts that walked and the beasts that crawled.

The trees, which could not move from where they grew, all turned their branches toward the Star. The tides stood still. Sea creatures bowed in prayer.

But no one had thought to tell the dove. She was alone in her home in the cliff, and not a single bird remembered her.

Too late, she learned about the Christ Child's birth. Too late, for He had disappeared. "They have taken Him to Egypt, to escape the soldiers," said the breezes.

The poor dove wept. She flew back and forth along the cliff, wringing her wings in grief. Her mournful cry brought echoes to the quiet valley.

"I will follow Him," she said at last. "For life is nothing if I cannot see His face!"

Down the valley flew the dove. Above the hills she flew, then westward up the caravan trail. And there her eyes were nearly blinded by the flash of sun on steel.

Below her marched the soldiers!

The dove flew onward, onward even through the night. And that was how she found them: two lonely travelers with a child, plodding through the darkness. Ahead of them, the trail turned both south and north across the plain.

The weary fugitives pushed southward.

But not the dove. She had a plan to save the child, and so she stayed behind, among the branches of a fig tree so different from the cliffs of home. She watched the small dark figures fade away.

Her mournful cry disturbed the stillness of the plain. She dared not follow them! Now she would never see His face.

"But neither will those soldiers," said the dove.

The sun was high; the soldiers came. They rested in the grove of trees. Above them mourned the dove.

"A dove!" a soldier cried. "What brings a dove out on the plain?"

"It is an omen," said another.

"An omen, but of what?" a third man asked.

The soldier shrugged. The others laughed —but no one quite forgot the bird's strange cry.

When the heat of the day had passed and the soldiers prepared to leave, the dove flew northward.

"The dove flies northward!" the leader shouted.

"It is indeed an omen!" cried the others. "The dove shows us the way."

She kept them with her for a day or two, leading them farther and farther from the fleeing child. And then she left them. Over the hills and above the valleys she flew, back to her home in the cliff.

For many years the poor dove mourned. She lived far longer than a dove is born to live. She was older than doves ever get to be, when a certain man came up the Jordan valley.

The breezes all around her said, "This is a holy man." But was it He? She flew along the riverbank to see.

The man was preaching, bathing people in the water as they knelt. But, no. This face was not the face she longed to see. The dove flew home again, to wait.

And one spring day He *did* walk up the valley. She
knew Him! He paused to ask the preacher something,
and the preacher seemed to know Him.

The dove flew down along the cliff. She raced across
the river just as He was wading into it. And then a strange
thing happened.

The dove began to feel as if on fire. "I am dying,"
she thought. "I have seen His face at last and I am
dying!"

For above Him the heavens had opened, piercing the dove with a terrible light. Her breathing stopped; she felt filled with a Spirit stronger than the very life within her.

"This is my beloved Son," the Spirit said, "in whom I am well pleased."

The light went out. The heavens closed. The dove
had disappeared.

But she had found Him! She had seen His face.

And it was through her frail and loyal body that the
Holy Spirit chose to sing His praise.